To Diane Camp
for always sharing her enthusiasm

Text and illustrations copyright © 2011 by Mo Willems
Elephant & Piggie is a trademark of The Mo Willems Studio, Inc.

Printed in the United States of America
Reinforced binding

First Edition, June 2011
20 19 18 17 16 15 14 13 12 11
FAC-034274-16077

Library of Congress Cataloging-in-Publication Data

Willems, Mo.
  Should I share my ice cream? / by Mo Willems. — 1st ed.
    p. cm. — (An Elephant & Piggie book)
  Summary: Gerald the elephant has a big decision to make, but will he make it in time?
  ISBN 978-1-4231-4343-7
[1. Sharing—Fiction. 2. Ice cream, ices, etc.—Fiction. 3. Friendship—Fiction. 4. Elephants—Fiction.
5. Pigs—Fiction.] I. Title.
  PZ7.W65535Sh 2011
  [E]—dc23   2011014860

Visit www.hyperionbooksforchildren.com and www.pigeonpresents.com

Should I Share My Ice Cream?

By Mo Willems

An ELEPHANT & PIGGIE Book

Hyperion Books for Children / *New York*
AN IMPRINT OF DISNEY BOOK GROUP

3

4

Should
I share my
awesome,
yummy,
sweet,
super,
great,
tasty,
nice,
cool
ice
cream?

20

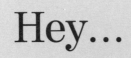

36

43

44

47

You look sad.
Would you like some
of my ice cream?

Elephant and Piggie have more funny adventures in:

Today I Will Fly!

My Friend Is Sad

I Am Invited to a Party!

There Is a Bird on Your Head!
(Theodor Seuss Geisel Medal)

I Love My New Toy!

I Will Surprise My Friend!

Are You Ready to Play Outside?
(Theodor Seuss Geisel Medal)

Watch Me Throw the Ball!

Elephants Cannot Dance!

Pigs Make Me Sneeze!

I Am Going!

Can I Play Too?

We Are in a Book!
(Theodor Seuss Geisel Honor)

I Broke My Trunk!
(Theodor Seuss Geisel Honor)

Happy Pig Day!

Listen to My Trumpet!

Let's Go for a Drive!
(Theodor Seuss Geisel Honor)

A Big Guy Took My Ball!
(Theodor Seuss Geisel Honor)

I'm a Frog!

My New Friend Is So Fun!

Waiting Is Not Easy!
(Theodor Seuss Geisel Honor)

I Will Take a Nap!

I *Really* Like Slop!